To

.... *Caleb* ....

WISHING YOU A VERY
MERRY
CHRISTMAS

Love from,

.... *Uncle Ben* ... *Aunt M...*
Carolyn & Charlie
2021

'Twas The Night Before
Christmas in
MICHIGAN

Illustrated by Jo Parry

HOMETOWN WORLD

Far, far away at the North Pole,
Santa is busy planning his Christmas Eve
journey across his favorite place...

Michigan!

MAP OF MICHIGAN

From Midland to Marquette,
from Detroit to Kalamazoo,
Santa can't wait to visit *all*
the children on his Nice List.

He piles his sleigh high with
a sack full of gifts, and *off he goes!*

As Santa soars over the Wolverine State,
he booms *"Hello!"* to Holland,
"Merry Christmas!" to Traverse City, and
gives Old Mission Peninsula a great big smile.

Suddenly, Santa spots the most important place of all:
"Are you ready for me to visit your home?"
he says with a hearty chuckle.

It's time to leave out a glass of milk and a plate of
sugar cookies, snuggle up in bed with
your favorite teddy, and *listen very closely...*

'Twas the night before Christmas,
when all through the house,
Not a creature was stirring,
not even a mouse;

The stockings were hung
by the chimney with care,
In hope that St. Nicholas
soon would be there.

You were nestled up all snug in your bed,
While visions of candy canes danced in your head.
And from Ann Arbor to the U.P., all across the map,
Children had settled down for a long winter's nap.

001

sleeps until santa visits

MICHIGAN

When out on the street
there arose such a clatter,
You sprang from your bed
to see what was the matter.

Away to the window
you flew like a flash,
Tore open the curtains,
threw open the latch.

The moon in the sky
with its full winter glow,
Shone bright as midday
on Michigan below.

When, what to your
wondering eyes should appear,
But a miniature sleigh
and eight tiny reindeer.

With a little old driver,
so lively and quick,
You knew in a moment
it must be St. Nick.
More rapid than eagles
his reindeer they came,
And he whistled, and shouted,
and called them by name:

"Now, Dasher! Now, Dancer!
Now, Prancer and Vixen!
On, Comet! On, Cupid!
On, Donder and Blitzen!
Take me up to the chimney; follow my call!
Now dash away, dash away, dash away all!"

And then, in a twinkling,
you heard on the roof
The prancing and pawing
of each little hoof.

As you pulled in your head
and were turning around,
Down the chimney
St. Nicholas came with a bound.

He was dressed all in fur,
from his head to his foot,
And his clothes were all tarnished
with ashes and soot.
A bundle of toys he had
flung on his back,
And he looked like a peddler
holding his pack.

His eyes–how they twinkled!
His dimples–how merry!
His cheeks were like roses,
his nose like a cherry.
His droll little mouth
was drawn up like a bow,
And the beard on his chin was
as white as the snow.

Dear Santa,
Welcome back to
Michigan!
I hope you enjoy the
yummy treats I have
left out for you.
Love from your
biggest fan!
xxx

He glanced at the names
that he held in his fist,
Children in Lansing and Grand Rapids
whom were next on his list.
He had a broad face
and a little round belly
That shook when he laughed,
like a bowl full of jelly.

He was chubby and plump,
a right jolly old elf,
And you laughed when you saw him,
in spite of yourself.
St. Nick winked an eye
and tilted his head,
Letting you know
you had nothing to dread.

He spoke not a word,
but went straight to his work,
And filled up your stocking,
then turned with a jerk.

And tapping his finger
at the side of his nose,
And giving a nod,
up the chimney he rose.

He sprang to his sleigh,
to his team gave a whistle,
And away they all flew
like the down of a thistle.
But St. Nicholas exclaimed,
as he drove out of sight–

THANK YOU Santa

Santa's magical journey is coming to an end.
He delivers the final gifts to Petoskey and Sault Sainte Marie,
waves goodbye to Mackinac Island, and laughs a
jolly *Ho-Ho-Ho* for everyone to hear.

Heading back home to his cozy workshop at the North Pole, Santa hopes each child is *extra* good next year...because he can't wait to come back to

Michigan!

Adapted from the poem by Clement C. Moore
Illustrated by Jo Parry
Designed by Ryan Dunn

Published by Hometown World,
an imprint of Sourcebooks Kids
P.O. Box 4410, Naperville, Illinois 60567-4410
(630) 961-3900
hometownworld.com
sourcebookskids.com

Date of Production: May 2021
Run Number: 5020473
Printed and bound in China (OGP)
10 9 8 7 6 5 4 3 2 1

To ....

CONGRATULATIONS

We are **SUPER** excited to inform you that
you made it onto the **NICE LIST**.
Keep up the good work and remember
to always be **KIND** and **MERRY**.
You are **TRULY** special.

Love,

Santa

and the elves
xXx